BEA'S 4 BEARS

For Dory and Charley
and their bears.

Clarion Books
a Houghton Mifflin Company imprint
215 Park Avenue South, New York, NY 10003
Text and illustrations copyright © 1992 by Martha Weston

Printed in Singapore

Library of Congress Cataloging-in-Publication Data

Weston, Martha.
Bea's 4 bears / by Martha Weston.
p.   cm.
Summary: By the end of her busy day Bea has gone from
having four teddy bears to having none, but by retracing her
steps she is able to get back up to four bears again.
ISBN 0-395-57791-8
[1. Teddy bears—Fiction.   2. Counting.]   I. Title.   II.
Title: Bea's four bears.
PZ7.W52645Be   1992   91-12529
[E]—dc20   CIP   AC

TWP 10 9 8 7 6 5 4 3 2 1

BEA'S 4 BEARS

MARTHA WESTON

Clarion Books • New York

This is Bea.

Bea has four bears.

She is taking them on a picnic,
but four bears don't fit in the wagon.

4 ⠶

Nighty Bear can stay with Bingo.

So Bea has three bears.

3

The picnic is delicious.

Oops! Silly Bear fell in her peanut butter!

Bea carefully washes her off…

and hangs her up to dry.

Now Bea has two bears.

Kay comes to play.

Kay wants to hold Heavy Bear.

2:

Bea says no…

but Kay can play with Dumpy Bear.

So Bea has one bear.

1.

Bea and Kay play bears-in-a-cave…

1.

until it's time for Kay to go home.

1.

Now, where are Bea's bears?

Bea has ZERO bears!

0

She is looking for them everywhere…

when she remembers
something important.

"Stop! You have Dumpy Bear!"

Here he is!

Now Bea has one bear!

1.

Bea sees two yellow feet.

1.

Yes! It's Heavy Bear!

Now Bea has two bears.

Silly Bear is dry—

so Bea has three bears.

Here comes Bingo with Nighty Bear.

3

At last! Bea has all four of her bears!

And she is glad.